This is dedicated to my family, a bunch of good *souls* who enable me to do it all.

FOREWORD

As a child, I can remember no greater feeling than putting on a new pair of back-to-school shoes. I can vividly recall the smell of the leather as I took them out of the box. From the moment I tied the laces, I felt as if I could run faster and jump higher.

For many children around the world, shoes are considered a luxury. I am proud to donate a portion of the proceeds from the sale of *Chocolate Shoes with Licorice Laces* to Soles4Souls. With each book sold, more children will tie their laces and jump as high as they can.

If you'd like to do a shoe drive in your school, please visit:

soles4souls.org

www.mascotbooks.com

Chocolate Shoes with Licorice Laces

For more information, please contact:
Mascot Books
560 Herndon Parkway #120
Herndon, VA 20170
info@mascotbooks.com

CPSIA Code: PRT0614A
ISBN-13: 9781620866658

Printed in the United States

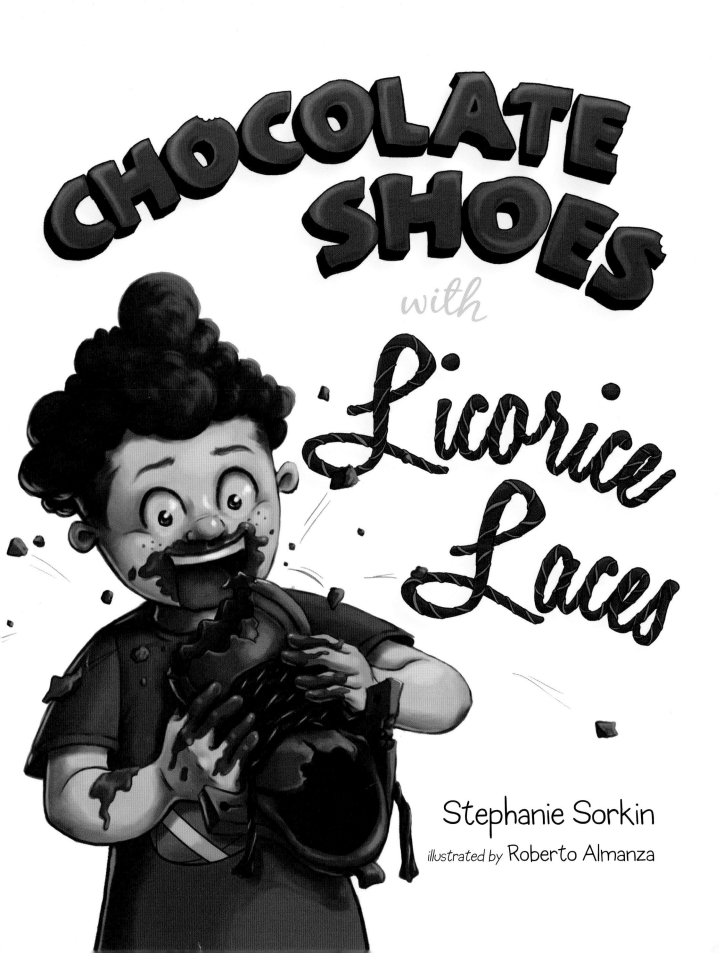

CHOCOLATE SHOES

with

Licorice Laces

Stephanie Sorkin

illustrated by Roberto Almanza

HELP! I don't know what to do!
My mom put me in chocolate shoes!

This must have been
A simple mistake.
What's next?
Will my shirt be a birthday cake?

I guess I shouldn't
Fuss and moan.

My sister's shoes are made

Of ice cream cones.

Clearly an error has been made.
I'll fix it while I relax in the shade.

These shoes of mine are awfully tight.
I think that I should take a bite.

Just a nibble,
No big deal.
I'll take a little
Off the heel.

It's not like I'm running
Relay races.
So I'll take a tiny taste
Of the licorice laces.

One bite,

two bites,

Three

and

four.

I can't stop eating

More and more.

Shoes for lunch!
Wow, this is fun!

yum yum y

yum yum

yum yum

My belly's full,

I'm feeling great.

I can't believe

What I just ate!

And soon it's just
My feet and me,
Lying under this shady tree.

CHOCOLATE SHOES

with Licorice Laces Treats

You will need:

Shoe-shaped cookie cutter
Shoestring red licorice
13x9 baking dish
1 cup flour
$\frac{1}{4}$ teaspoon baking soda
$\frac{1}{4}$ teaspoon salt
$\frac{3}{4}$ cup sugar
$\frac{1}{2}$ cup butter
2 tablespoons water
8 ounces semi-sweet chocolate
2 eggs
2 teaspoons vanilla

1) Preheat Oven to 350 degrees.

2) Mix flour, baking soda, and salt in a small bowl and set aside.

3) Melt sugar, butter, and water in a saucepan on the stovetop.
   Remove from heat.

4) Slowly add pieces of chocolate and stir to melt. Add entire mixture to a bowl.

5) In a separate bowl, blend eggs. Add vanilla and then add flour mixture.

6) Combine the two mixtures together in one bowl and mix well.

7) Pour into a greased 13x9 baking pan.

8) Bake for 15-20 minutes. Start checking at 15 minutes with a toothpick to see
   if it is thoroughly cooked.

9) When cool, cut into shoe-shaped pieces with a cookie cutter.
   Decorate with licorice to replicate shoelaces.
   Makes six shoe-shaped treats.

Food allergies? Recipe can be easily adjusted! For gluten-free treats, substitute flour with gluten-free flour. For an egg-free option, use one 6 ounce container of Greek yogurt in place of the eggs. For a dairy-free option, use Parve margarine in place of the butter and Parve chocolate. This recipe is peanut and tree-nut free, assuming that you check the manufacturing practices of all the ingredients.

No cookie cutter? Use a round drinking glass, cut brownies into circles, and decorate with licorice. Still adorable and always delicious!

Short on time? Use a brownie mix and prepare as per directions on the box.

ENJOY!

ABOUT THE AUTHOR

Stephanie Sorkin lives in New York with her husband and three children. She is a member of the Society of Children's Book Writers and Illustrators. Stephanie is the author of the award-winning book, *Nutley, the Nut-Free Squirrel*, which she donates 100% of the proceeds to F.A.R.E. Stephanie's next title, *Frenemy Jane, the Sometimes Friend*, will be released in the fall 2014.